Karen's New Friend

Look for these
and other books about Karen
in the
Baby-sitters Little Sister series:

1 Karen's Witch
2 Karen's Roller Skates
3 Karen's Worst Day
4 Karen's Kittycat Club
5 Karen's School Picture
6 Karen's Little Sister
7 Karen's Birthday
8 Karen's Haircut
9 Karen's Sleepover
#10 Karen's Grandmothers
#11 Karen's Prize
#12 Karen's Ghost
#13 Karen's Surprise
#14 Karen's New Year
#15 Karen's in Love
#16 Karen's Goldfish
#17 Karen's Brothers
#18 Karen's Home Run
#19 Karen's Good-bye
#20 Karen's Carnival
#21 Karen's New Teacher
#22 Karen's Little Witch
#23 Karen's Doll

#24 Karen's School Trip
#25 Karen's Pen Pal
#26 Karen's Ducklings
#27 Karen's Big Joke
#28 Karen's Tea Party
#29 Karen's Cartwheel
#30 Karen's Kittens
#31 Karen's Bully
#32 Karen's Pumpkin Patch
#33 Karen's Secret
#34 Karen's Snow Day
#35 Karen's Doll Hospital
#36 Karen's New Friend
#37 Karen's Tuba

Super Specials:
1 Karen's Wish
2 Karen's Plane Trip
3 Karen's Mystery
4 Karen, Hannie, and
     Nancy: The Three
     Musketeers
5 Karen's Baby

Little Sister

Karen's New Friend
Ann M. Martin

Illustrations by Susan Tang

A
LITTLE APPLE
PAPERBACK

SCHOLASTIC INC.
New York Toronto London Auckland Sydney

This book is for Leigh and Allison —
Welcome!

ISBN 0-590-45651-2

12 11 10 9 8 7 6 5 4 3 2   3 4 5 6 7 8/9

Printed in the U.S.A.   40

First Scholastic printing, March 1993

The New Kid

One Friday morning, my teacher wrote two words on the blackboard. She wrote them in capital letters, like this:

HANDICAPPED
DISABLED

Then she left them on the board. She opened her attendance book.

"I wonder what she is doing?" I said to Hannie and Nancy.

Hannie Papadakis and Nancy Dawes are

my two best friends. I am Karen Brewer. Hannie and Nancy and I call ourselves the Three Musketeers. We are so lucky that we get to be in Ms. Colman's second-grade class together. Not all best friends can be in the same classroom. And not every teacher is as wonderful as Ms. Colman. Ms. Colman is patient. Ms. Colman is funny. Ms. Colman is full of surprises. Ms. Colman hardly ever yells. When *we* yell, she just reminds us to use our indoor voices. (Ms. Colman is going to get married soon.)

Before my friends and I could figure out why Ms. Colman had written those words on the board, the bell rang. We scrambled for our seats. Nancy and Hannie sit next to each other in the back row. I have to sit in the front row. That is because I wear glasses. (I even have two pairs. The blue pair is for reading. The pink pair is for the rest of the time. Except for when I am asleep, of course.) Ms. Colman likes for the glasses-wearers to sit up front, near the blackboard. I sit between Natalie Springer and Ricky Torres. Ricky is my pretend husband. We got married on the playground one afternoon.

Ms. Colman took attendance. We listened to the morning announcements. Then our teacher pointed to the board. "Who can read these words?" she asked us. "Can you sound them out?" We sounded them out. "Who knows what they mean?" she asked.

"When you can't walk?" suggested Natalie.

"That is one kind of handicap," said Ms. Colman. Then she added, "A person who is blind or deaf is handicapped or disabled, too."

We talked about people who cannot do some things as well as most other people can. Then Ms. Colman said, "Boys and girls, on Monday a new student will join our class. Her name is Addie. She has cerebral palsy and she cannot use her legs. She uses a wheelchair instead."

"The new kid is a *girl*?" said Bobby Gianelli. He made a face. "Our last new kid was a girl. This room has too many girls. The boys are outnumbered!"

I raised my hand. "Where is Addie moving from?" I asked.

"Oh, she lives here in Stoneybrook," Ms. Colman replied. "She is just switching schools. She did not move."

Then Nancy raised her hand. "What is cerebral palsy?" she wanted to know.

"When a person has cerebral palsy," said Ms. Colman, "her brain has trouble sending messages to some parts of her body. That is why Addie cannot use her legs to walk or run, like you can. But the rest of Addie is fine. She can use her hands. She can read and write. She can laugh and sing and tell jokes. I hope you will make Addie feel welcome on Monday. It is not easy being the new kid in school."

I remembered our last new student, Pamela Harding. Pamela is a snob. She turned out to be my best enemy. Addie just had to be nicer than Pamela. I wondered what

Addie looked like. I wondered what she liked to do. I wondered so much that I had a little trouble paying attention to Ms. Colman. I had even more trouble after lunch. That is because I was thinking about the weekend. It was a big-house weekend, and I was excited.

2

Hawaii

A big-house weekend is a weekend at Daddy's. See, I live in two houses, Mommy's little house and Daddy's big house. That is because my parents are divorced. They do not live together anymore. A long time ago, they used to be married. Then we all lived in the big house — Daddy, Mommy, me, and Andrew. (Andrew is my little brother. He is four going on five.) But after awhile Mommy and Daddy decided they did not love each other anymore. They loved Andrew and me very much, but not

6

each other. So they divorced. Daddy stayed in the big house. (He grew up there.) Mommy moved to the little house. She brought Andrew and me with her. The little house is not far from the big house. Both of them are in Stoneybrook, Connecticut.

After awhile an interesting thing happened. Mommy and Daddy got married again, but not to each other. Mommy married Seth. Now he is my stepfather. Daddy married Elizabeth. Now she is my stepmother.

Here are the people in my little-house family: Mommy, Seth, me, Andrew. Plus some pets. We have three. Rocky and Midgie are Seth's cat and dog. Emily Junior is my rat.

Here are the people in my big-house family: Daddy, Elizabeth, Nannie, Andrew, me, Kristy, Sam, Charlie, David Michael, and Emily Michelle. Our pets are Shannon, Boo-Boo, Crystal Light the Second, and Goldfishie. Nannie is Elizabeth's mother, so she is my stepgrandmother. Kristy, Sam, Charlie, and David Michael are Elizabeth's kids, so they are my stepsister and stepbrothers. (Elizabeth was married once before she married Daddy.) Sam and Charlie are big. They go to high school. David Michael is seven like me. Well, actually, he is a few months older, which is important to him, but not to me. Kristy is thirteen, and she is a baby-sitter. I just love Kristy. She is the best big sister I could ever have. She plays with me and takes care of me. And when I am at the little house, she calls me on the phone. Emily Michelle is my adopted sister. She is two and a half. Daddy and Elizabeth adopted her from the country of Vietnam, which is very far away. Mostly Emily is okay, but sometimes she is a pain. (I named my rat after her.) Shannon is David Michael's puppy, and Boo-Boo is Daddy's fat old tomcat. Crystal Light the Second and Goldfishie are goldfish. (What a surprise.) They belong to Andrew and me.

8

Usually, Andrew and I live at Mommy's house. But every other weekend and on some vacations and holidays we live at Daddy's. We also live at Daddy's whenever Mommy and Seth take a vacation. And very soon they were going to Hawaii for two weeks. They had been waiting and waiting for that trip. So had Andrew and I. We just love being at the big house. We could not wait to live there for two weeks. We feel very special at Daddy's.

Do you know what I call my brother and me? I call us Andrew Two-Two and Karen Two-Two. (I got the idea for those names after Ms. Colman read our class a book called *Jacob Two-Two Meets the Hooded Fang*.) We are two-twos because we have two houses and two families, two mommies and two daddies, two dogs and two cats. Plus, I have two stuffed cats — Goosie at the little house, Moosie at the big house. I have toys and books and clothes at each house. I have my two best friends — Nancy at the little house, Hannie at the big house. And of course I have those two pairs of glasses.

My big-house weekend was going to be gigundoly fun. I would not even mind leaving on Sunday. That was because Andrew and I would go right back on Friday for two whole weeks.

3

The Fire

The big-house weekend was fun. It was perfect. On Saturday afternoon, Kristy took me to the movies. Just us sisters. On Saturday evening, everyone was at home for dinner. Afterward, Daddy and Elizabeth let us make our own ice-cream sundaes. Then on Sunday (the day, not the dessert), I went to Hannie's house. We played with our Barbies.

After awhile, Hannie said, "This year I decided to make my valentines."

"Me, too," I said. "And it is a good thing

11

Valentine's Day will not be here for awhile. Think of all the cards I have to make. Eleven, just for the people in my two families. Then there are all the kids in our class."

"Plus Ms. Colman," added Hannie. "Don't forget Ms. Colman."

"Oh, I wouldn't," I replied. "Not ever. I have to make Ms. Colman an extra special Valentine's Day card."

"So do I," said Hannie.

But we were not sure what to make.

I was still thinking about Ms. Colman's card when I went back to the big house for lunch. Maybe I would make a card out of felt. Or maybe I would make a gigundo card, as tall as Ms. Colman. I liked the idea of a tall card a lot. When lunch was over I decided I better phone Hannie to tell her about it.

I reached for the phone and — *Ring, ring!*

I picked it up right away. So did someone else.

"Hello?" I said.

"Hello?" said Elizabeth. She must have answered the phone upstairs.

"Elizabeth?" said the voice.

"Colleen?" cried Elizabeth. "Hi, honey!"

Colleen is Elizabeth's sister. I have met her a couple of times. Like at the wedding when Daddy and Elizabeth got married. Colleen lives in Massachusetts (I think). She is married to a man named Wallace. Colleen and Wallace are Kristy's aunt and uncle. (And Sam's and Charlie's and David Michael's.) They have four children named Ashley, Berk, Grace, and Peter. I have met the kids, too. At the wedding and one other time. But I do not remember them very well.

"Elizabeth," Colleen began. She sounded kind of chokey.

"What's wrong?" asked Elizabeth. "Something is wrong. I can tell."

"There was a fire in our house last night."

"Oh, no! Was anyone at home?"

"No," said Colleen. "Thank goodness."

"Wait a sec," said Elizabeth. "I'm going to put Watson on the cordless phone. I want him to hear this, too." (Watson is Daddy.)

No one told me to get off the phone in the kitchen, so I did not. (Actually, I do not think anyone knew I was on.)

"Watson?" said Elizabeth. "Colleen is on the phone. They had a fire in their house last night."

"I'm so sorry," said Daddy. "What happened?"

"We are not sure how the fire started," Colleen replied. "But it caused a lot of damage. The house can be repaired. It will take awhile, though. And we cannot live in it now. We spent last night with our neighbors. The kids are just starting a two-week school vacation — "

Daddy interrupted Colleen then. "Come stay with us," he said. "Spend the vacation here. There is room for everyone. Karen

14

and Andrew will be here next week, too. But that is okay."

"Oh, thank you!" said Colleen. "We will come tomorrow."

Goodness, I thought. You just never know what to expect.

4

Adelaide

On Monday morning, Seth drove Nancy and me to school.

"Today we meet Addie," I reminded Nancy. "The new girl."

We wondered what Addie looked like. We wondered what her wheelchair looked like. We wondered many things. We did not have to wait long to find out about them.

When Nancy and I reached our classroom, Hannie was already there. So were some other kids. So was Ms. Colman. So were Addie and her mother and another teacher. I did not know the other teacher's name, but I had seen her around school.

Sure enough, Addie was sitting in a wheelchair. It was not a big wheelchair for grown-ups. It was just Addie's size. A tray rested across the front of the wheelchair, over Addie's knees. I guessed that was her desk. Addie's wheelchair would not fit under any of the desks in the room. Slung over the side of the wheelchair was a big tote bag. Addie could carry things with her wherever she went.

Do you know what? Addie's chair and the tray and even the tote bag were covered with stickers. Stickers, stickers everywhere. Fuzzy stickers, glittery stickers, puffy stickers. Stickers that were words and pictures and designs. I had never seen so many stickers in one place.

Addie was sitting up tall in her chair. She was talking to Ms. Colman. She looked like any other girl in our class. She was wearing sneakers and jeans and a baggy shirt. Her dark hair was tied with a red ribbon.

I watched as Ms. Colman showed Addie where she would sit. Then Addie wheeled herself to the aisle between Ricky's desk and the windows. She set the brake on her chair. She found two pencils in her tote bag and put them on her tray. She was ready for school.

Addie's mother kissed her good-bye. She left the room. Ms. Colman went to the blackboard. The other teacher moved to the back of the room. My friends and I settled down. We kept glancing at Addie.

After the morning announcements, Ms. Colman said, "Boys and girls, our new student has joined us today. Addie, would you like to tell us a little about yourself?"

"Okay," said Addie. She did not sound shy. In fact, she moved her chair to the front of the room so she was facing everyone. "My name is Adelaide Sidney," she began. "Everyone calls me Addie. I used to go to Stoneybrook Elementary. I like to write poems and draw and read, and I collect stickers. I have one brother and one

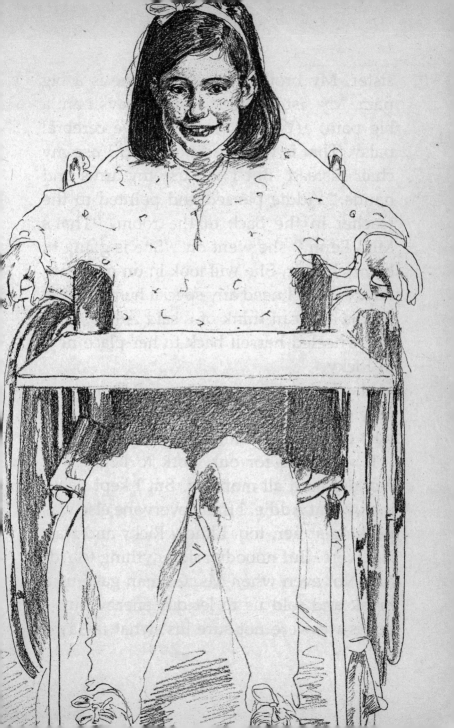

sister. My brother is nine and he is a big pain. My sister is four and she says *I* am a big pain." (We laughed.) "I have cerebral palsy. That is why I cannot walk. I use my chair instead. But I can use my arms and hands." Addie paused and pointed to the teacher in the back of the room. "That's Miss Penn," she went on. "She is going to be my helper. She will look in on me every day to see if I need any special help. I guess that is all I can think of," said Addie. And she wheeled herself back to her place next to Ricky.

Ms. Colman smiled at her. "Thank you very much, Addie. All right, class. Please take out your reading books."

It was time for our work to begin. We worked hard all morning. But I kept peeking over at Addie. I think everyone else was peeking at her, too. I know Ricky and Natalie were. But nobody said anything to Addie. Not even when Ms. Colman gave us a break and told us to let our energy out. I guess we were not sure just what to say.

20

5

Recess

All morning Addie sat in her wheelchair and worked at her tray. Everything she needed was in her tote bag — her pencils, her erasers, her paper, even a book to read. Her tote bag was like the inside of my desk.

Addie raised her hand a lot. I think she liked her new school.

At lunchtime, our class lined up to walk to the cafeteria. Addie lined up with us. She was right in front of me. When Ms. Colman led us into the hall, Addie pushed herself along in her chair. Miss Penn asked her if she needed help getting through the doorway, but Addie said, "No, thank you," and she did it herself.

The Three Musketeers sat together at one of the long tables in the cafeteria. We try to sit together whenever we can. That is what best friends do.

"Where will Addie sit?" I whispered to Hannie. "I do not think she can sit on these benches."

Hannie and Nancy and I watched Addie. Miss Penn was showing Addie that she could sit at the end of our table where there was no bench. Addie did not even need the table anyway. She ate on her tray.

Ricky Torres was sitting next to me. He leaned over and whispered in my ear, "I wonder what Addie eats for lunch."

"She eats what anyone eats, stupid," I told him.

But I watched Addie to make sure I was right. We were all watching Addie. We watched her open her lunch bag. We watched her take out an apple, a sandwich, and a juice box. We watched her bite into the sandwich.

After awhile I whispered to Nancy, "Do you think Addie can go outside for recess? What can she do on the playground?"

Nancy did not know. But I got an answer to my question anyway. When my friends and I were finishing our lunches and getting ready for the playground, Ms. Colman came to our table. She whispered something to Addie. Addie nodded. Then she cleaned off her tray. She followed Ms. Colman out of the cafeteria. I think they were going back to our classroom.

"Poor Addie," I said. "She cannot play on the playground."

At recess, the Three Musketeers stood together by the monkey bars. After awhile, Natalie Springer joined us. Then Ricky and Bobby and Hank Reubens came over. So did Pamela Harding and her friends Jannie and Leslie. So did Terri and Tammy, the twins.

"I did not know Addie would be able to

push her*self* in her wheelchair," said Leslie. "I thought Miss Penn would push her."

"Addie's arms must get tired," I said.

"She is very good at spelling," said Ricky. "I looked at her worksheet."

"If I were Addie, I would not like to sit down all the time," said Terri.

"How do you think she goes to the bathroom?" asked Jannie.

"Maybe that's what Miss Penn helps her with," said Tammy.

"Who here thinks Addie is nice?" asked Pamela. "Raise your hand."

A couple of kids started to raise their hands. Then they put them down.

"Who here thinks she is weird?" asked Pamela.

Not one hand was raised. Except for Pamela's.

"I think she is weird," she said.

"She is not!" I cried. "Addie is not weird! She just cannot walk. Anyway, Pamela, don't you feel sorry for Addie? I do. Terri is right. Addie has to sit down all the time.

That is no fun. She cannot even come outside for recess. We should all be nice to Addie. I am going to be extra nice to her from now on."

Pamela stuck her tongue out at me. "You do not know everything, Karen Brewer," she said. "Even though you think you do."

I stuck my tongue out at Pamela. I crossed my eyes at her, too. Then I said to Nancy and Hannie, "Come on. Let's play by ourselves."

We left Meanie Pamela behind.

I promised myself I would be a good friend to Addie.

6

Addie's Best Friend

While I was on the playground with my friends, I had an idea. It was an idea about Addie, and it was a good one.

"You guys," I said to Nancy and Hannie, "I just got an idea. I have to go inside right away. I have to ask Ms. Colman something."

"What?" asked Nancy. "What do you have to ask her?"

"I cannot tell you now. I don't have enough time. The bell is going to ring any second. I will tell you later." I had already turned around. I was running across the playground.

When I reached my classroom, Ms. Colman was sitting at her desk. She was all alone. Addie was not there.

"Ms. Colman," I called. (I was out of breath.)

"Indoor voice, Karen," she reminded me.

"Sorry," I said quietly. "Ms. Colman, where is Addie? I have an idea."

"She is with Miss Penn," said my teacher.

"Oh. Ms. Colman, I have decided I want to be Addie's partner."

"Her partner?"

"Her — special helper. Miss Penn will not be here all the time, and Addie might need help. I could push her chair when her arms get tired. I could get things for her that she cannot reach. Plus, Addie is new in school. I could show her where the library is, and the nurse's office, and the supply closet, and anything else."

"Well, Karen, that would be nice," said Ms. Colman. "That is very thoughtful. I am sure Addie would appreciate it. Let's talk to her when Miss Penn brings her back."

So we did.

Miss Penn and Addie came back just as recess was ending. Everyone poured into the room at once. Ms. Colman took Addie and me aside. "Addie," she said. "Karen has offered to be your helper. Would you like that? She can show you around, and give you a hand if you need it."

"I can get things for you when Miss Penn isn't around," I added. "I am good at bending over or jumping up. I have a lot of energy. Everyone says so. And I could push you in the hallway when it is crowded."

Addie smiled at me. "Okay!" she said. "That would be great. Thanks, Karen."

I smiled back. "You're welcome!"

"Karen," said Ms. Colman, "to be Addie's helper, you should sit next to her. So why don't you switch seats with Ricky."

"Okay. Hey, Ricky! We are switching seats!" I yelled. (Ricky was standing right next to me, but I was a little excited.)

29

So Ricky said, "Indoor voice, Karen."

Then Ms. Colman helped us switch our desks around. That was easier than trying to get all Ricky's stuff out of his desk and into mine. I have never seen so much junk. Ricky is a packrat.

All afternoon I sat next to Addie and helped her. When she dropped her pencil, I picked it up. When she needed her eraser, I pulled it out of her tote bag. When Ms. Colman told us to write some numbers on a piece of paper, I checked Addie's work. When Ms. Colman told us to take our spelling books home, I said to Addie, "That is your *blue* book."

"I know," she replied.

"Here, I will get it for you."

"I can get it," said Addie.

But I reached into her bag first.

The bell rang then. School was over. "I enjoyed being your helper," I told Addie. "And I am looking forward to tomorrow." I paused. Then I added, "I am going to be your very best friend, Addie."

Ms. Colman's Wedding

While we were putting on our coats, three different kids said to me, "You are going to be Addie's best friend, Karen?" (I guess I had not been using my indoor voice when I told Addie that.)

"Yes, I am," I replied proudly. *Some*body in our room had to be nice to Addie, and I guessed it was me.

That afternoon, Mrs. Dawes drove Nancy and me home. Nancy sat in front with her mother. I sat in back with Danny. Danny is Nancy's new baby brother. He sleeps a lot, especially when he is in the car.

The ride to the little house was very quiet. Danny was asleep. No one was talking. I did not like so much quiet.

"Nancy?" I said. Nancy did not answer. "Nancy?" I said again. ". . . Nancy? Calling Nancy Dawes."

"What is it?" Nancy did not laugh. She did not even turn around.

I paused. "Are you in a bad mood?" I finally asked.

"No."

Nancy did not say anything else. Her mother pulled into the driveway. I did not want to go next door to the little house. Not yet. Not until I knew what was wrong with Nancy.

Nancy and I climbed out of the car. We watched Mrs. Dawes lift Danny out of his seat. Then Nancy turned away. "Well, 'bye," she said to me.

"Nancy, wait!" I caught the sleeve of her jacket. "What is the matter?" I asked her. "Are you mad at me?"

"Of course I am," she answered.

"But why?"

"Because you want Addie to be your new best friend."

"I do not!" I cried. "I said I am going to be *Addie's* best friend. But you and Hannie are *my* best friends."

"Oh," said Nancy. "Then never mind."

Nancy and I giggled. We were friends again. (I was not even sure if we had actually had a fight. But it did not matter anyway.)

I spent the afternoon at Nancy's house. First we played with Danny. We pretended we were his baby-sitters. Mrs. Dawes let us change his diaper. Then we went to Nancy's room to talk.

"Maybe," I said, "after Ms. Colman gets married, she will have a baby."

"Like Danny," added Nancy. "Do you think she really will?"

I shrugged. "Lots of people have babies after they get married. But not everybody. You know what? Ms. Colman already has a whole classful of kids."

"I wonder what her husband is like," said Nancy.

"You mean her fiancé," I corrected her. "He is not her husband yet. He will not be her husband until after the wedding."

"Her fiancé then," said Nancy. "I am sure he is very nice."

"*I* wonder what he will give her for Valentine's Day."

"Something extra, extra special," said Nancy dreamily. "Since they are in love."

"I wish we could meet Ms. Colman's fiancé," I added. "I would like to know who Ms. Colman is marrying."

When Nancy and I got tired of talking, we played with Danny some more. Then I had to go home for supper.

That night I thought about Addie. I wondered how I would feel if I could not use my legs. How would I go up and down our stairs? Would someone have to carry me? What would I do outdoors on nice days? Would I ever be able to go swimming? Or build a snowman? Could I ride on a sled? What would I do if I were downstairs and Andrew were upstairs, and he yelled, "Hey, Karen! Come here!"?

I told myself once again that I had to be very, *very*, VERY nice to Addie.

Karen the Helper

"Here I am! Your helper and your best friend," I announced.

It was Tuesday morning. I was back in school. Addie had just wheeled herself into Ms. Colman's room. I ran to her. I did not want her to forget who I was. I was going to be very important to Addie.

Addie smiled. "Hi, Karen," she said. She headed into the room.

I grabbed the back of her chair. I pushed Addie toward her place by my desk.

"Wait!" said Addie. "I have to go to my

cubby first. I have to take off my coat and put my stuff away."

"Oh, I will do those things for you," I said. I pushed Addie next to my desk. I watched her set the brake on her chair. Good. Now I knew how to do it. I could take care of that for her from now on.

I helped Addie take off her coat. Then I ran to her cubby and hung it up for her. Addie began to follow me.

"Where are you going?" I asked her.

"I have to put away my scarf and mittens, too."

"I'll do that!" I called gaily. "That is what I am here for."

When I had put Addie's things away, I ran back to her. "Now what should I do?" I asked. "Just name it and I will do it."

"Nothing, thank you," said Addie. She reached for her tote bag.

"Here! Let me!" I cried. I reached into the bag for her. "What do you need?"

"My spelling book and two pencils." I

handed them to Addie. She looked at the pencils and frowned. "Uh-oh. Where is the pencil sharpener?" she asked. "I better sharpen these."

"Never fear! I will do it!"

"But I can — " Addie started to say.

Too late. I had already grabbed those pencils. I sharpened them quick as a wink. Then I handed them back to Addie.

"Thanks," she said quietly. After a few minutes she added, "I could have done that myself. I really could have." She glanced toward the back of the room. "I can reach the pencil sharpener."

"Well, you can just count on me," I replied.

At lunchtime I sat near the end of one of the long tables. I sat by Addie. Nancy sat next to me, and Hannie sat across from me.

Addie looked out the windows of the cafeteria. She looked at the playground. The

sun was shining brightly. "I cannot wait to go outside," she said.

"To go outside?" I repeated. "You mean, after school?"

"No, at recess."

"You are going onto the playground?" I asked. "I thought you had to stay inside."

"No way!" exclaimed Addie.

"But you stayed inside yesterday."

"Miss Penn had to give me a reading test. That was all."

Oh. What was Addie going to *do* on the playground? I wondered. But I did not ask her. I did not think that would be polite.

When lunch was over, I pushed Addie outside. Then we hung around together. I had to stay with Addie. That was my job. Besides, I was her best friend. If I did not stick with her, what would she do?

"Karen?" said Addie. "You can go play with the other kids. I don't care." Addie pointed across the playground. Hannie and

Nancy were waving to me from the monkey bars.

"Oh, that is okay," I told Addie. "I will stay with you."

"I have a book to read," said Addie. "It is right here in my bag."

"That is okay," I said again.

I stood next to Addie until recess was over.

9

Going to the Mall

Being Addie's helper was a big job. It kept me busy. It even made me a little tired. Ms. Colman thought I was working too hard. She kept saying things like, "Karen, Addie can sharpen her own pencils." And "Karen, Addie can find her spelling book. She knows what it looks like."

Finally on Thursday Ms. Colman pulled me aside before school began. I was rooting through Addie's tote bag. I was finding two pencils for her. I did that every morning so Addie would be ready for the day.

"Karen," said Ms. Colman, "please do not do everything *for* Addie, okay? I told you that yesterday."

"Okay," I replied. "Sorry."

Still, I felt bad for Addie. The other kids did not talk to her very much. So it was up to me to be nice to Adelaide Sidney.

I felt especially sorry for Addie on Friday. In the morning, before school began, everyone was talking about the weekend.

"Hey, Jannie!" I heard Pamela say. "Are you coming skating with me?"

"Sure!" replied Jannie. "Leslie's coming too. She got new skates."

"Hey, Natalie," said Terri. "My mom said you can come over for lunch tomorrow. Tammy and I are going to make spaghetti all by ourselves with only a little help. We can have a spaghetti feast."

"Thanks!" said Natalie.

"I am going to a birthday party this afternoon," announced Bobby. "My cousin invited me, and he said I could bring a friend. Want to come, Ricky?"

"Okay," said Ricky.

Everyone was inviting everyone else to go somewhere, or to do something. But no one was inviting Addie. No one was near her. No one was even looking at her. Addie was just sitting in her chair. She was reading a book by Mr. Edward Lear. She was laughing at the funny poems. But I felt bad for her because she was going to have such an awful, boring weekend.

So all morning I was extra, extra nice to Addie. Even though Ms. Colman had asked me not to be so helpful. Then, on the playground, I stood around next to Addie again. She kept looking in her tote bag at Mr. Lear's book. She was probably afraid I was going to leave her all alone and then she would be stuck reading by herself. But I would never do that.

After awhile Addie said, "What are you doing this weekend, Karen?"

"Going to my father's house," I said.

"My brother and I are going to stay there for two weeks. My stepcousins will be there, too."

"Oh."

I realized that Addie probably did not have any plans for the weekend. So I said, "Addie, I could come over to your house tomorrow. I could read to you or something. I would not mind."

"Thanks," said Addie, "but I can read to myself. Besides, I am going to go to the mall with my friends."

She was? Addie was going to the mall?

"What friends?" I asked her.

"My friends at home. The ones in my neighborhood. My friends from my old school. Four of us are going. Our mothers take us pretty often. Maybe once a month."

"What do you do there?" I asked.

"Everything," Addie replied. "We shop. Sometimes we go to a movie. We eat lunch in a restaurant. Once, we all got our ears pierced. Tomorrow we are going to the pet store because Barbara is going to pick out a parakeet for her birthday. Barbie is my best friend."

Well, for heaven's sake. Addie was going to the mall. Addie had friends. Addie even had a best friend. And her best friend was not me.

The Relatives
Take Over

"Has everyone been to the bathroom?" asked Mommy.

"Yes!" said Andrew and I.

"Is everything you need in the car?" asked Seth.

"Yes!" said Andrew and I.

"Are you buckled up?" asked Mommy.

"Yes!" said Andrew and I.

It was Friday afternoon. Mommy and Seth were ready for their trip to Hawaii. Andrew and I were ready to go to the big house for two weeks. We had been to the bathroom. We were packed. We were buckled into our seats. I was holding Emily Junior's cage on my lap. She was coming with us. Rocky and Midgie were not. Our neighbor was going to take care of them. I would miss Rocky and Midgie.

Seth drove us to Daddy's house. He helped us out of the car.

"You two behave yourselves," Mommy said to Andrew and me. "And have fun," she added.

"We will miss you," said Seth.

"Same here," I replied. "Bring me a lei from Hawaii. 'Bye!"

Andrew called good-bye, too. Then he began to cry. But he stopped as soon as we were inside Daddy's house. Everyone was there to greet us — our big-house family plus Colleen and Wallace and their kids, Ashley and Berk and Grace and Peter. Guess how many people were standing in the living room and the hallway. Sixteen, including Andrew and me.

The house was stuffed.

At first I did not know what to do.

Then Ashley stepped forward. "I am Ashley Miller," she said. "Remember me? I am ten years old. I am your stepcousin."

"And I am Grace Miller," said Grace. "I am six, almost your age. Let's go upstairs." Grace pulled me toward the steps.

"You can stay in our room," said Ashley as we ran upstairs. She led me into *my* room.

"*Your* room?" I exclaimed. "But — "

"Here. I can help you unpack," said Grace. "Then I should go downstairs again. I was helping Nannie with dinner."

That is *my* job, I thought.

At dinnertime we had to eat at two tables. Andrew and I sat at the kitchen table with Ashley, Grace, Berk, Peter, David Michael, Emily, and Kristy. (Kristy was helping the littlest kids.) Everyone else ate in the dining room.

"Isn't this fun?" said Kristy. "One huge happy family."

No. I thought. It is not fun. But then I remembered that the Millers' house had

49

burned down. So I should be nice to them.

When dinner was over, Daddy said, "How about a treat tonight, everybody? Let's go to the Rosebud Cafe for ice cream."

"Yes!" I cried.

There were too many of us to fit in Daddy's van. Charlie took some people in his car, the Junk Bucket. He took Kristy, Berk, Peter, Andrew, and me.

"I call I get to sit next to Kristy!" I said.

But Berk was already sitting next to her.

At the restaurant, Berk sat next to Kristy again. Grace sat on her other side.

"Can I sit in your lap?" I asked.

"While we both eat ice cream?" replied Kristy. "I do not think that would work."

I sat at a different table. I could not even *see* Kristy.

"We sure are a crowded family," Andrew whispered to me.

"The relatives are taking over," I whispered back. I reminded myself about the fire. But I still wanted to sit next to Kristy.

11

"We Have to Be Nice"

When we returned to the big house, Daddy said, "Bedtime for the younger kids, and you know who you are." He meant everyone ten and under.

Ashley took my hand. "Let's go, Karen."

"Yeah, let's go, Karen," said Grace.

They pulled me upstairs.

"Where is your nightgown, Karen?" asked Grace. "I will get it for you."

"I can get it," I said. But Grace got it anyway.

Then Ashley hung up the clothes I had been wearing.

"I could have done that," I said.

"No problem!" replied Ashley.

I sat on my bed. I looked around my room. It did not look like my room anymore. Grace's suitcase was open on the floor. Ashley's clothes spilled out of my closet. Two strange stuffed animals sat on my bed with Moosie. (Moosie did not look happy.)

"Whose are those?" I asked. I pointed to the animals.

"Mine," said Grace. "But you can sleep with them tonight."

"That's okay. I sleep with Moosie," I told her. I rescued Moosie from the strange animals. I patted his head. Then I went into the bathroom.

Ashley and Grace followed me.

"I have to brush my teeth," I told them.

"We will help," said Grace. She un-

screwed the top of the toothpaste. She handed me my toothbrush.

"I can do it myself!" I cried.

"I was just — " Grace started to say. But Ashley poked her.

After that, no one said anything until we were back in the bedroom.

I looked at my bed and the two cots next to it.

"You can sleep in the bed," said Ashley.

"But I was sleeping in it!" exclaimed Grace.

Hmphh. It was *my* bed.

"Grace," Ashley whispered loudly. "Don't be a pain. Remember, we have to be nice to Karen. Her parents are divorced, and she lives in two houses. She has to go back and forth, back and forth."

I do not think I was supposed to hear what Ashley said. But I had heard anyway. I felt my cheeks grow hot. I could not look at my stepcousins.

For heaven's sake, what was wrong with divorced parents? It is no big deal. Lots of kids' parents are divorced. Anyway, at least I *had* two houses. Ashley did not even have one house, because it had burned up. I did not say that, though. I just climbed into my bed and pretended to fall asleep. I also pretended that Ashley and Grace were not in the room.

12

Escape!

When I woke up on Saturday morning, the first thing I saw was Grace. The second thing I saw was Ashley. One in each of the cots. They were still asleep. Good.

Very, very slowly and carefully I climbed out of bed. I tiptoed across the room. I did not want to wake up Grace and Ashley. I was afraid they would offer to feed me my breakfast or brush my teeth for me.

Tippity-tippity-toe. I got out of that room in a hurry.

Downstairs I ate breakfast. I ate with Andrew and Nannie. We were the only ones up. I hoped no one else would get up for awhile. I chewed my cereal quietly. And I tried not to clink my spoon against the bowl.

Soon I heard voices, though. Ashley and Grace and Berk and Peter all ran into the kitchen at the same time.

"Good morning, Karen," said Ashley. "Did you sleep well?"

"Yes," I said, and I dashed out of the kitchen. I raced to my room, got dressed, and raced downstairs again. "I'm going to Hannie's house!" I yelled. Then I raced across the street.

"Hannie!" I cried, when she let me inside. "I have to escape! Can I hide here?"

"Of course," said Hannie. She led me to her room. "What are you escaping from? Should I close my door?"

"And lock it," I told her. "I am escaping from my relatives. They have taken over everything. Plus, Ashley and Grace treat me like a baby who cannot do anything for

58

herself. And Grace is younger than me! Also, she sleeps with her mouth open and kind of snores all night."

"Ew," said Hannie.

"So I need to stay over here for awhile." I got up and tiptoed to the window. I peeped outside. Then I pulled the shade down.

"Are they out there?" whispered Hannie.

"No. Not yet. But I am not taking any chances."

"What are you going to do later?" asked Hannie.

"What do you mean?"

"Well, you can stay here for lunch, but you will have to go back sometime."

I sighed. "I know." Hannie and I were quiet for awhile. Then I said, "Guess what Addie is doing today."

"What?"

"She is going to the mall with her friends from her old school." (I did not say that one of them was her best friend.) "I wish

I could go to the mall today," I added. "With*out* the relatives."

"What is Addie going to do at the mall?" wondered Hannie.

"Shop and have lunch," I told her.

"Just like we do," said Hannie thoughtfully. "You know what? I think Addie is nice. I am glad she is in our class."

"Me, too. But I have to work very hard to be her helper."

"Ms. Colman says you are working too hard."

"I know. Hey, guess what. I started making my valentine for Ms. Colman."

"So did I!" Hannie showed me the card she was working on.

"I just wish I knew what her fiancé was giving her," I said.

"Maybe he will give her a ruby ring! A ruby-red ring for Valentine's Day. Wouldn't that be romantic?"

"Very. Do you think her fiancé is romantic?"

"Yes. And handsome," said Hannie. "I am sure he is handsome. And I bet he has some important, exciting job."

"Oh, we just *have* to find out about him," I said. But we did not know how to do that. So we sat in Hannie's room and wondered about him. That was better than going back to the big house.

13

The Big Fight

On Monday I arrived at school extra early. That was because of my stepcousins. I had needed to escape from them again. So I had run to Hannie's house as soon as I got dressed. Mrs. Papadakis said I could stay for breakfast. Then I asked if she could take us to school before Ashley found out where I was. So far, Ashley and Grace had not come over to Hannie's house. I wanted to keep it that way.

Hannie and I were the first kids to arrive in our classroom.

"Ah. Peace and quiet," I said.

But soon the room was busy and noisy. That was okay. As long as Ashley and Grace were not around.

When Addie showed up, I ran to her.

"Hi! Hi, Addie!" I called. "Did you have fun at the mall?"

"Tons!" she answered. "I bought a pack of glow-in-the-dark stickers. And a pair of earrings. We are going back next weekend."

Addie was wheeling herself toward her cubby.

"I'll push you," I said.

"I can do it," said Addie.

But I pushed her anyway. I pushed her over to her spot by my desk.

"Karen, I have to go to my *cubby*," said Addie. "I have to hang up my coat."

"I will do it for you."

Addie did not answer. She just sighed. Then she took off her coat and handed it to me. While I was hanging it up, Addie went to the pencil sharpener. I ran across the room and grabbed her pencils. Boy, did Addie ever keep me busy. I stuck the pencils in the sharpener.

"Karen," said Addie, "I can do it my*self*."

"I am supposed to be your helper," I replied.

"Okay. But you do not have to help me so much."

Our day began. Ms. Colman made some announcements. We had Show and Share, and Addie showed us her stickers. Everyone liked them, even Pamela. Pamela said they were cool.

When it was time for spelling, Ms. Colman said, "Okay, boys and girls. Please take out a pencil and a piece of paper."

I reached into Addie's tote bag to find her paper.

"Leave me alone, Karen!" Addie whispered loudly. "Just leave me alone!"

I glanced at Ms. Colman. She was busy writing on the blackboard. "I am trying to be nice to you," I hissed.

"Well, stop it!"

Hmphh. What was wrong with Addie? I reached into my desk for my own pencil and a piece of paper.

Addie leaned over to me. "I am not a baby, you know," she said.

Well, for heaven's sake.

"Addie — " I began. But Ms. Colman turned around then.

"Are you ready, boys and girls?" asked our teacher.

During spelling I stared straight ahead at Ms. Colman. I did not look at Addie. Not once. Not even when she dropped her pencil on the floor. (Bobby Gianelli picked it up for her.)

When spelling was over I said, "Do you know what, Addie Sidney? You are a big pain. I am not going to be your helper anymore."

"Good," said Addie. "I do not *want* you to be my helper."

"Girls?" said Ms. Colman. "What is going on?"

"I am not Addie's helper anymore," I

answered. "Someone else can have that job."

"I do not *need* a helper!" exclaimed Addie.

"Please calm down," said Ms. Colman. Then she let Ricky and me switch our seats again. We were back in our old places. I refused to look at Addie.

14

The Mystery Man

At lunchtime, Nancy and Hannie and I did not sit in our usual seats. "I want to be as far away from Addie as possible," I said.

We sat at one end of the long table and Addie sat at the other end. Natalie and the twins sat near her. I could hear them talking. They told Addie about the spaghetti feast. Addie told them some more about the mall.

"Do you like spaghetti?" Tammy asked Addie.

"I love it," said Addie.

"Well, the next time we have a spaghetti feast, maybe you could come, too."

"Thanks!" said Addie.

When Addie had finished her lunch, she wheeled herself to the door to the playground. The lunchroom monitor held it open for her. Then he helped her roll over the bump in the doorway.

Addie disappeared outside.

"I wonder what she will do today without you," said Hannie.

"Oh, who cares," I replied.

"What was your fight about?" Nancy wanted to know.

"Nothing."

"But you and Addie are really mad at each other."

"So what? It is none of your business." Uh-oh. I sounded mad at Nancy, too. "Sorry," I said. I did not want to start another fight.

Nancy sighed. "That's okay. I guess."

My friends and I finished our lunches. We put on our coats. We went outside. I looked around for Addie. She was all by herself. She was bundled up in her chair, parked on the blacktop where kids play four-square and hopscotch and jumprope. She was reading a book.

"Come on, you guys," I said to Hannie and Nancy. I led my friends toward the monkey bars, far away from Addie Sidney.

"Where are we going?" asked Hannie.

"Away from Addie. I am ignoring her," I announced.

I did not *really* ignore her, though. I kept peeking at her during recess. I wanted to know what she would do without me around.

For awhile, Addie just read. Nancy and Hannie and I hung from the monkey bars and talked about Ms. Colman's fiancé.

"Maybe he has an exciting job like . . . a detective. Yeah, maybe he is a detective," suggested Hannie. "I just know he does something interesting."

"Maybe he is a spy!" exclaimed Nancy.

"Nope. Too dangerous," I decided. "Maybe he is a pilot."

I looked across the playground. Addie had put her book away. She had moved over to a bunch of girls from the other second-grade class. She was watching them play hopscotch.

Terri and Tammy wandered over to the monkey bars. They listened to us talk about Ms. Colman's fiancé.

"Maybe he is a horse trainer," said Terri.

Hannie shrugged. "He is a Mystery Man."

Natalie wandered over. Then Pamela and Jannie wandered over.

(I checked on Addie. She was talking to a teacher.)

"We need to find out about the Mystery Man," said Pamela after awhile. "But how?"

"*We* could be spies!" I cried. "We could follow Ms. Colman after school."

"Or we could assign Ms. Colman to write a composition," suggested Natalie. "She always makes us write them. She would have to call it 'All About My Husband.' "

I giggled. "You cannot make your teacher do homework," I said.

"I know," replied Natalie. "I was just having fun."

That was true. We all were. I think even Addie was having fun — without me.

"Leave Me Alone!"

Guess who picked up Hannie and me at school that afternoon. Charlie. He came in the Junk Bucket.

"Hi, Charlie!" I called.

"Hi!" he replied.

"Hi!" said two more voices.

Boo and bullfrogs. Ashley and Grace were in the car, too. They were both sitting in the front seat with Charlie. But when they saw me, they scrambled out. "You can sit up front, Karen," said Ashley.

So Hannie and I crawled into the front.

My stepcousins slid into the back. "Who is your friend?" Ashley asked me.

I did not want to tell her. I did not want her to invade Hannie's house the way she had invaded mine.

When I did not answer, Charlie nudged me with his elbow.

"She's Hannie," I said to Ashley.

Charlie glared at me. "Her name is Hannie Papadakis and she lives across the street," he told Ashley. "She is one of Karen's best friends."

"Karen, how nice," said Ashley.

"Do you and Hannie want to play with me and Ashley?" asked Grace.

"No, thanks," I said. "Um, we have too much homework."

Actually, we did have some homework. Ms. Colman hardly ever gives us homework, but that evening we were supposed to write a little story about what kind of pet we would have if we could have any pet in the whole wide world. I was going to write about a monkey.

Since I had told Ashley and Grace about my homework I had to start it right away. Ashley and Grace left me alone. They said I should work in peace. Even so, the story was not easy to write. By dinnertime, I had not finished it.

At the supper table, Grace spread my napkin on my lap for me. Ashley poured my milk. I pointed out that I was seven years old, but maybe she did not hear me. She cut up my chicken for me, too. Later, Grace served me dessert.

I was glad when I was able to say, "Well, I have not finished my homework yet. I am going back to my room."

I was almost finished with the monkey story when someone knocked on my door.

"Come in," I said.

Ashley poked her head into the room. "Are you still working?" she asked. She stepped inside and peered at my paper.

"Yes," I replied.

"You must be getting tired," she said. "Let me finish that for you."

"My story?" I cried. "No! I can do it my-self. Leave me alone!"

"Sorry," said Ashley.

I did not say, "That's okay." I just stood up and grabbed my story. Then I finished it in Kristy's room.

Soon, it was bedtime. When Ashley and Grace and I were changing out of our clothes, Grace held my nightgown toward me. "Let me help you," she said.

"No!" I howled. I yanked the nightgown from her. I pulled my quilt and pillow off my bed. Then I ran into the playroom. "And don't follow me!" I yelled to my stepcousins.

In the playroom, I put the quilt and pil-low on the couch. I would spend the night there. I did not need a bed. Besides, all the animals were in the playroom. The goldfish were in their tank. Emily Junior was in her cage. Shannon and Boo-Boo were napping on the floor. They would be much better company than Ashley and Grace.

Ashley and Grace

I woke up slowly the next morning. My mind woke up first, before my eyes did. It is Tuesday, I thought. Five more days until the relatives leave. Finally I opened my eyes. I saw an aquarium and a cage and a TV set and shelves full of toys. I was not in my room. Where was I?

Then I remembered. The playroom. I had had a fight with Grace and Ashley. I was sleeping on the couch. Boo-Boo was sleeping on my stomach, and Shannon was sleeping by my feet.

After a few minutes, I heard a whisper.

"Karen?" said a soft voice. "Karen, are you awake?"

Grace and Ashley were standing in the doorway. They were wearing their night-gowns. Their hair was all messy.

"I'm awake," I said.

"Can we talk to you?" whispered Ashley.

"Okay."

Ashley and Grace ran into the room in their bare feet.

"I'm freezing!" cried Grace.

"Get under the quilt," I said. "It is warm in here."

Ashley and Grace and I huddled under the quilt. Boo-Boo ran off. He looked annoyed. But Shannon stayed with us.

"Karen," said Ashley, "we are sorry we made you mad. We were only trying to be nice to you. Honest."

"I know," I replied. "But I heard what you said about the divorce. I do not want you to be nice to me because my parents are divorced. I want you to be nice because you like me. Also, I do not need you to do everything for me. I am not a baby."

"No. You're not," agreed Ashley. "We really are sorry, Karen."

"Really," added Grace. "We promise not to do all those things for you. But we still want to be your friends. Do you want to be ours?"

I thought for a moment. Then I said, "Yes."

"Good," replied Ashley. "I have an idea. How about if we start over? Let's pretend that you and Andrew just got here, and the last few days never happened. How is that?"

"It's fine," I said. I paused. Then I went on, "Hi, Ashley! Hi, Grace!"

"Hi, Karen!" my stepcousins answered. "So glad you could come!"

17

Karen and Addie

I liked starting over. That was a gigundoly wonderful idea. Maybe Addie and I could start over, too. While my stepcousins and I got dressed that morning, I thought about some of the things we had said to each other. I thought about Ashley and Grace being nice to me because I am a divorced kid. I think actually they had felt sorry for me. Then I thought about Addie. Had I tried to be her friend because I liked her or because she has cerebral palsy? Maybe I felt sorry for her, too. Plus, I had treated Addie like a baby, just the way Ashley and Grace had treated me. That was not a way to make a new friend. I guess Addie knew it. Now so did I. I did not know if Addie would forgive me, but maybe we could start over.

When Hannie and I reached Ms. Colman's room that morning, we hung up our coats in our cubbies. Then I marched over to Addie Sidney.

"Addie," I said, "I am very, very sorry about our fight. And I am sorry I was so helpful. I guess I really was not helpful at all."

"I am sorry I got mad," replied Addie. "But you know, I *can* do lots of things myself. I just need help with *some* things."

"Do you still want to be friends?" I asked Addie.

She nodded. "Yes. But Karen, I do have other friends. And Barbie is my very best friend. I think she always will be."

"That's okay. Hannie and Nancy are *my* best friends. You know what? I think we should start over. Let's pretend this is your first day in our class. I will stay in my old seat. And I will be your helper, but only when you really need a helper."

So Addie and I started over. I did not do every little thing for her. Twice I asked her if she needed help. Once she did and once she did not. At lunchtime, Hannie and Nancy and I went back to our usual seats in the cafeteria. I waited to see where Addie would sit. She sat with us.

When lunch was over, I said, "Addie, do you want help going outside?"

"I just need help getting through the door," she answered.

So Nancy held the door open, and I pushed Addie through.

"Well, the Three Musketeers are now going to the monkey bars," I announced.

"Wait, Karen," said Addie. "What do you and the other kids talk about over there every day?"

"Mostly about Ms. Colman's fiancé."

"Ms. Colman is getting married?" asked Addie.

84

"Yes," replied Hannie. "To a Mystery Man."

"We are trying to find out more about him," explained Nancy.

"Can I come with you?" asked Addie.

"Of course," I replied.

"Great! I just need a little help getting there."

That day almost our whole class gathered by the monkey bars. Even the boys were curious about the Mystery Man.

"He could be a great explorer," said Hank.

"He could be an astronaut," said Bobby.

"Or even a mail carrier," said Natalie.

"How will we ever find out?" wondered Leslie.

"Why don't we ask Ms. Colman if we could invite him to our class?" suggested Addie.

My friends and I looked at each other. Why hadn't we thought of that? It made much more sense than spying on Ms. Colman.

"That is a great idea!" cried Pamela. "Who should ask her?"

Now we all looked at Addie. "Would you do it?" I said.

"Sure," replied Addie. "Right after recess is over."

18

Friendship

As soon as we were sitting at our desks in Ms. Colman's room, Addie raised her hand. She did not look nervous at all.

"Yes, Addie?" said our teacher.

"Ms. Colman, we were wondering," began Addie. "I mean, all of us were wondering." Addie looked around at my classmates and me.

"Wondering what?" asked Ms. Colman.

"Wondering about the man you are going to marry. Your fiancé."

"Mr. Simmons," said Ms. Colman.

"That is who you are marrying?" asked Addie. "Mr. Simmons?"

Ms. Colman nodded. "Mr. Henry Simmons."

"Well, we decided he is probably very nice," Addie went on. "And we would like to meet him. Do you think he could come to school one day?"

"Certainly," said Ms. Colman. She smiled. "Would you like to make an invitation for him? An invitation from all of you?"

"Yes!" we cried.

"All right. Let's do that now. I will help you. What shall we say?"

I raised my hand. "The invitation should start 'Dear Mr. Simmons.' "

"Okay," said Ms. Colman. She wrote that on the blackboard. "Then what?"

Ricky raised his hand. "We would like to meet you. Please come visit our class." Then he added, "As soon as possible."

Ms. Colman wrote those sentences on the board.

Natalie raised her hand. "Put down 'We want to know if you are a mail carrier or an explorer or what?'"

I raised my hand again. "Ask him if he can come on Friday," I said. "I do not think we can wait much longer."

When the invitation was finished, Addie copied it onto a piece of paper. She wrote all the words on one side of the paper. On the other side of the paper we signed our names. Then Ms. Colman gave me some crayons and I colored very beautiful flowers around the borders.

"That is lovely," said Ms. Colman when I handed the invitation to her. "I will give it to Mr. Simmons after school today."

Then Ms. Colman collected our stories about pets. She read them to herself while we wrote another composition.

"The title of this composition is Friendship," said Ms. Colman. "You may write anything you want about friendship — a poem, a story, a play, or an essay."

Ms. Colman gives us lots of writing work.

Luckily, I love to write. And I had plenty to say about friendship. I decided to write an essay.

I wrote: Friendship is being nice to someone because you like her. Friendship is helping someone, but not too much. Friendship is letting someone be herself. A good friend is not bossy. A good friend knows how to listen. You can always tell a secret to a good friend. By Karen Brewer.

When I finished my essay I dedicated it to Addie. I wrote "To Addie From Karen" across the top. Then I showed the paper to Ms. Colman.

"Ms. Colman?" I whispered. "When you are done with this, may I please give it to Addie? I dedicated it to her."

"Why don't you give it to her now?" Ms. Colman whispered back.

"Okay. Thanks."

I walked around to Addie's chair. I handed her the paper. "This is for you," I said. "You can have it."

Addie read my essay. "Thank you, Karen!" she exclaimed.

"Thank *you*," I replied.

"For what?"

"For helping us find out about Mr. Henry Simmons. Soon he will not be the Mystery Man."

19

Mr. Henry Simmons

On Thursday Ms. Colman said, "Boys and girls, tomorrow Mr. Simmons will visit us. He is going to come in the afternoon. He will stay for half an hour before the end of school. What would you like to do while he's here?"

"Ask him lots of questions," said Hannie.

"Make his visit extra special," I said.

"How shall we make it special?" asked Ms. Colman.

"Let's have a party!" cried Bobby.

"We will have some refreshments," said

Ms. Colman. "But I do not think we need to have a party."

"Maybe he would like to see some of our work," said Pamela.

"Our friendship stories!" I shouted.

"Indoor voice, Karen," Ms. Colman reminded me. "I think that is a good idea. Who would like to put the stories on the bulletin board?"

Terri and Tammy took the job. (They got to use the stapler.)

The rest of us colored a big sign that said WELCOME, MR. SIMMONS. We each colored one letter. When we finished, we decided we were ready for Mr. Simmons' visit. We could not wait.

By Friday afternoon the bulletin board was finished. Our welcome sign was hanging over the blackboard. On Ms. Colman's desk were a box of cookies, a bottle of juice, a stack of napkins, and a stack of cups. Ms. Colman's chair had been moved to the front of the room. Jannie Gilbert had decorated it with crêpe paper. We were sitting quietly at our desks. We were wearing name tags.

We were ready to meet Mr. Henry Simmons.

When someone knocked on the door to our room, I shrieked.

"He's here!" I cried.

Ms. Colman opened the door. A man walked into our room. He was very tall. He was wearing a raincoat and a hat.

"Do you think he is an astronaut?" I whispered to Ricky.

Ricky shook his head. "I do not think so."

"Boys and girls," said Ms. Colman, "I would like you to meet my fiancé, Henry Simmons. Henry, this is my class."

"Good afternoon," said Mr. Henry Simmons. "I am very happy to meet you. I have heard a lot about you. Thank you for your invitation."

Mr. Simmons took off his coat and hat. He sat in the special chair. Addie wheeled herself over to him. She gave him a paper

flower she had made. Then Terri stood up. She gave a speech.

"Welcome," she said. "We have been very busy writing stories and essays. Yesterday we wrote about friendship. Now we will read to you."

Terri, Hank, Pamela, Bobby, and Ricky read their stories. Then I read my essay, the one I had dedicated to Addie. After that, it was time for questions and answers.

Natalie raised her hand. "I do not want to be nosy," she said to Mr. Henry Simmons, "but what do you do?"

"I am the principal at a high school," he answered.

A few kids looked a little disappointed. I knew they wanted Mr. Simmons to be something exciting. But a school principal was okay with me.

I raised my hand. "Do you live nearby?" I asked.

"Pretty nearby," said Mr. Simmons.

"So after you and Ms. Colman get married, you won't move away?"

"We will not move away. I promise. Ms. Colman will still be your teacher."

I decided I liked Mr. Henry Simmons. When the bell rang and he had to leave, I was sorry to see him go.

The Good-bye Party

On Saturday morning I woke up in my room at the big house. I was not sleeping in my bed. I was sleeping on one of the cots. Ashley and Grace and I had been trading the bed around.

It was almost time for the Millers to leave. Sunday would be their last day with us. They had to go back to their own house. Ashley and Grace and Berk and Peter needed to start school again. Their house was not as good as new, but at least they could live in it again. Ashley said the repairmen had been working on it all week. She said she was going to get new furniture for her bedroom. She also said she missed her old furniture. She looked a little sad.

"I *liked* my old furniture," she told me. "I do not like the way new furniture smells. My old furniture was perfect."

"You know what?" I said. "I think we should have a party tonight. A going-away party for you and your family."

"Yeah!" cried Ashley.

"Let's talk to Kristy," I said.

Ashley and I talked to Kristy, and Kristy talked to the grown-ups. The grown-ups said we could have a party. They said they would take care of the food if we would take care of the entertainment.

Ashley and Grace and I decided to put on a play. We wrote it ourselves. We called it "Super Girls From Mars." We made Emily Michelle play an outer-space puppy.

At six o'clock that night the doorbell rang.

"The pizza is here!" I yelled. Everybody

else must have been as excited about the party as I was, because no one told me to use my indoor voice. They just raced to the door to get the pizza.

Guess what. Elizabeth and Nannie had set the table in the kitchen and the table in the dining room as if we were going to have a fancy dinner party. We ate the pizza from china plates. We drank milk and soda from goblets.

After dinner, Ashley and Grace and Emily and I put on our play.

"We are proud to present 'Super Girls From Mars,'" I announced.

Grace forgot her lines and Emily's puppy ears kept falling off, but no one minded. When the play was over, everyone clapped.

After that, all the boys sang a song. (Well, they did not really sing. They just moved their lips while some people on a CD sang.) Then the adults wanted to play charades, but the kids did not. We watched a video and ate popcorn instead.

When the video was over, so was the

party. Daddy said it was bedtime.

On Sunday morning I felt sad. I watched Ashley and Grace pack their suitcases. "You know what?" I said. "I am going to miss you."

"You will?" said Grace. "We will miss you, too."

"Maybe we could write to each other," I said. "I like to get mail."

We decided to be pen pals.

When breakfast was over, the Millers loaded up their car. They climbed inside. Nobody wanted to say good-bye, but we had to anyway.

"Drive safely!" said Daddy.

"Wear your seatbelts!" called Andrew.

"Call us when you get there!" said Elizabeth.

"Good-bye! Good-bye, everyone!" I shouted. "Come again soon!"

"Good-bye, Karen!"

I watched the Millers' car pull into the street. Then I went inside with my big-house family.

About the Author

ANN M. MARTIN lives in New York City and loves animals, especially cats. She has two cats of her own, Mouse and Rosie.

Other books by Ann M. Martin that you might enjoy are *Stage Fright*; *Me and Katie (the Pest)*; and the books in *The Baby-sitters Club* series.

Ann likes ice cream and *I Love Lucy*. And she has her own little sister, whose name is Jane.

Little Sister

Don't miss #37

KAREN'S TUBA

When we reached the music room I looked for the row of instruments under the blackboard. All I saw were chairs. And a tuba in the corner.

"Well, what's left?" I asked Mrs. Dade.

She pointed to the tuba.

"That's *it*? Where's the flute? I thought the flute would be here."

"Someone in the other second-grade class chose it," said Mrs. Dade.

"You mean I have to play the *tuba*?" I exclaimed.

"Well — " Mrs. Dade began to say.

But I could not hear the rest of her sentence. My classmates were giggling.

LITTLE ® APPLE ®

B·A·B·Y·S·I·T·T·E·R·S

Little Sister ®

by Ann M. Martin, author of *The Baby-sitters Club* ®

☐	MQ44300-3	#1	Karen's Witch	$2.75
☐	MQ44259-7	#2	Karen's Roller Skates	$2.75
☐	MQ44299-7	#3	Karen's Worst Day	$2.75
☐	MQ44264-3	#4	Karen's Kittycat Club	$2.75
☐	MQ44258-9	#5	Karen's School Picture	$2.75
☐	MQ43651-1	#10	Karen's Grandmothers	$2.75
☐	MQ43650-3	#11	Karen's Prize	$2.75
☐	MQ43649-X	#12	Karen's Ghost	$2.75
☐	MQ43648-1	#13	Karen's Surprise	$2.75
☐	MQ43646-5	#14	Karen's New Year	$2.75
☐	MQ43645-7	#15	Karen's in Love	$2.75
☐	MQ43644-9	#16	Karen's Goldfish	$2.75
☐	MQ43643-0	#17	Karen's Brothers	$2.75
☐	MQ43642-2	#18	Karen's Home-Run	$2.75
☐	MQ43641-4	#19	Karen's Good-Bye	$2.95
☐	MQ44823-4	#20	Karen's Carnival	$2.75
☐	MQ44824-2	#21	Karen's New Teacher	$2.95
☐	MQ44833-1	#22	Karen's Little Witch	$2.95
☐	MQ44832-3	#23	Karen's Doll	$2.95
☐	MQ44859-5	#24	Karen's School Trip	$2.75
☐	MQ44831-5	#25	Karen's Pen Pal	$2.75
☐	MQ44830-7	#26	Karen's Ducklings	$2.75
☐	MQ44829-3	#27	Karen's Big Joke	$2.75
☐	MQ44828-5	#28	Karen's Tea Party	$2.75
☐	MQ44825-0	#29	Karen's Cartwheel	$2.75
☐	MQ45645-8	#30	Karen's Kittens	$2.75
☐	MQ45646-6	#31	Karen's Bully	$2.95
☐	MQ45647-4	#32	Karen's Pumpkin Patch	$2.95
☐	MQ45648-2	#33	Karen's Secret	$2.95
☐	MQ45650-4	#34	Karen's Snow Day	$2.95
☐	MQ45652-0	#35	Karen's Doll Hosital	$2.95

Pssst... Know what? You can find out **everything** there is to know about *The Baby-sitters Club*. Join the BABY-SITTERS FAN CLUB! Get the hot news on the series, the inside scoop on all the Baby-sitters, and lots of baby-sitting fun...just for $4.95!

With your **two-year** membership, you get:

 ☆ An official membership card!
 ☆ A colorful banner!
 ☆ The exclusive Baby-sitters Fan Club quarterly newsletter with baby-sitting tips, activities and more!

Just fill in the coupon below and mail with payment to:
THE BABY-SITTERS FAN CLUB,
Scholastic Inc., P.O. Box 7500, 2931 E. McCarty Street, Jefferson City, MO 65012.

The Baby-sitters Fan Club

❏ **YES!** Enroll me in The Baby-sitters Fan Club! I've enclosed my check or money order (no cash please) for $4.95 made payable to Scholastic Inc.

Name _____ Age _____

Street _____

City_____ State/Zip _____

Where did you buy this *Baby-sitters Club* book?

❏ Bookstore ❏ Drugstore ❏ Supermarket ❏ Book Club
❏ Book Fair ❏ Other_____(specify)
Not available outside of U.S. and Canada.

BSC791

It's a Super Special Month!

YOU CAN WIN A TRIP TO WALT DISNEY WORLD RESORT®!

Enter The Winter Super Special Giveaway for The Baby-sitters Club® and Baby-sitters Little Sister® fans!

Visit Walt Disney World Resort...and experience all the excitement of Peter Pan, Tinkerbell, and a whole cast of characters! We'll send the **Grand Prize Winner** of this Giveaway and his/her parent or guardian (age 21 or older) on an all-expense paid trip, for 5 days and 4 nights, to Walt Disney World Resort in Florida!

10 Second Prize Winners get a Baby-sitters Club Record Album!
25 Third Prize Winners get a Baby-sitters Club T-shirt!

Early Bird Bonus!
100 early entries will receive a Baby-sitters Club calendar! But hurry!
To qualify, your entry must be postmarked by December 1, 1992.

Just fill in the coupon below or write the information on a 3" x 5" piece of paper and mail to:
THE WINTER SUPER SPECIAL GIVEAWAY, P.O. Box 7500, Jefferson City, MO 65102.
Return by March 31, 1993.

Rules: Entries must be postmarked by March 31, 1993. Winners will be picked at random and notified by mail. No purchase necessary. Valid only in the U.S. Void where prohibited. Taxes on prizes are the responsibility of the winners and their immediate families. Employees of Scholastic Inc.; its agencies, affiliates, subsidiaries; and their immediate families are not eligible. For a complete list of winners, send a self-addressed stamped envelope after March 31, 1993 to: The Winter Super Special Giveaway Winners List, at the address provided above.

- -

The Winter Super Special Giveaway

Name _____ Age _____

Street _____

City _____ State/Zip _____

Where did you buy this book?

☐ Bookstore   ☐ Drugstore   ☐ Supermarket   ☐ Library
☐ Book Club   ☐ Book Fair   ☐ Other_____(specify)   BSC692